The Phantom Lollipop Lady

and Other Poems

ADRIAN HENRI

Illustrated by Tony Ross

D1637667

MAMMOTH

First published in Great Britain 1986
by Methuen Children's Books Ltd
Magnet edition first published 1987
Reprinted 1988
Published 1989 by Mammoth
an imprint of Mandarin Paperbacks
Michelin House, 81 Fulham Road, London SW3 6RB
Reprinted 1990

Mandarin is an imprint of the Octopus Publishing Group

Text copyright © 1986 Adrian Henri
Illustrations copyright © 1986 Tony Ross
ISBN 0 7497 0227 3
Printed in Great Britain
by Cox & Wyman Ltd, Reading

For Spike Sterne

Noble Jones from Wallasey, the bravest cat in the world

Noble Jones is noble
Noble Jones is strong
Noble Jones goes round the place
Defending right from wrong
A smile upon his noble face
Embodiment of feline grace
He's the pride of Merseyside
The bravest cat in the world.

A gang of desperadoes
Had terrorized the land
There were ugly scenes in Milton Keynes
Till Noble took a hand

He hounded them in Hounslow
And tied some up in Tring
He caught the rest in Crawley
They couldn't do a thing

Single-pawed he beat them
At their evil game
Locked them up in Wormwood Scrubs
And wouldn't leave his name.

For Noble Jones is modest
And Noble Jones is strong
Villains quake and start to shake
When Noble comes along.

Relaxing at New Brighton
Curled up on the beach
He saw a kitten drowning
Swept from her parents' reach

Swiftly to the rescue
He sprang into the waves
Avoiding by a whisker
A hero's watery grave

Safely from the Mersey
He set her on the shore
But when the crowd turned round to cheer
He'd disappeared once more.

For Noble Jones is modest
And Noble Jones is shy
People cheer, forget their fear
When Noble passes by.

One day at Watford Junction
The brakes refused to function
And the Inter-City nearly left the track

With no fear of broken bones
Down jumped brave Noble Jones
Dug in his claws and hauled the engine back.

As big as a crocodile's toothbrush
As huge as dinosaur's bones
As large as an elephant's hanky
Is the heart of Noble Jones.

In Cardiff and Carmarthen
They sang his praise aloud
From Penrith down to Plymouth
They did our hero proud

When The Queen conferred his Knighthood
A banner was unfurled
SIR NOBLE JONES FROM WALLASEY
THE BRAVEST CAT IN THE WORLD.

For Noble Jones is noble
and Noble Jones is strong
Noble Jones goes round the place
Defending right from wrong
A smile upon his noble face
Embodiment of feline grace
He's the pride of Merseyside
The bravest cat in the world.

Cargoes

Where are you going to
All you container-trains,
Where are you going to,
Please tell me where?

Where are you going to
All you container-ships,
Where are you going to?
Please take me there.

Penguins to Portslade
Boulders to Biggleswade
Butane to Bootle
and bedclothes to Ware.

Camels to Clunbury
Golfballs to Sunbury
Teacakes to Bunbury
not Aberdare.

Cardgames to Cardiff
Carports to Newport
Stockpots to Stockport
and coals to Kildare.

Cats to Kilkenny
and Abergavenny
Diamonds (not many:
we can't tell you where).

Gravestones to Gravesend
Wallflowers to Wallsend
Shampoo to Southend
and Barnet Fair.

Camshafts to Camberley
Tin cans to Timperley
Biscuits to Shrewsbury
and County Clare.

That's where we're going to
Said the container-trains,
That's where we're going to,
We've told you where.

That's where we're going to
Said the container-ships,
That's where we're going to,
We'll take you there.

The Lurkers

On our Estate
When it's getting late
In the middle of the night
They come in flocks
From beneath tower-blocks
And crawl towards the light

Down the Crescent
Up the Drive
Late at night
They come alive
Lurking here and lurking there
Sniffing at the midnight air

Up the Shopping Centre
You might just hear their call
Something like a bin-bag
Moving by the wall

Lurking at the bus-stop
Seen through broken glass
Something dark and slimy
Down the underpass

On our Estate
When it's getting late
In the middle of the night
There are things that lurk
About their work
Till dawn puts them to flight.

Domestic Help

The other day,
one of our domestic robots went mad,
kissed my dad,
poured marmalade over the videowall,
shampooed the cat,
sugared my mother's hair,
and sat on my sister's knee
(she fell through the chair).

Dad's frantic fiddling with the control-panel
only made matters worse.

It vacuum-cleaned the ceiling,
put the coffee-table into the garbage disposal unit,
uncorked a bottle of wine
and poured it gently over the carpet,
then carefully unscrewed its head
and deposited it in Mum's lap.

Mother says
that's the way it is these days:
you can't get the robots you used to.

Marigolds

I bought a bottle of Nettle Shampoo
this morning.
When I got home I wondered whether
I shouldn't shampoo
the marigolds
as well.

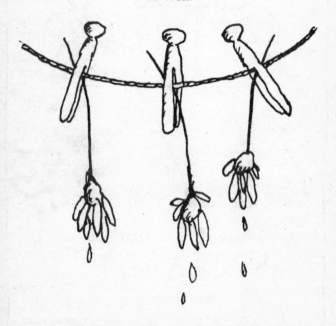

A Poem for my Cat

You're black and sleek and beautiful
What a pity your best friends won't tell you
Your breath smells of Kit-E-Kat.

Telephones

Grownups
Never stop complaining about the telephone
'It's been ringing all day'
they say,
but never leave it alone.

They moan all the time
'I can't get any work done'
'Wouldn't it be fun
without one?' So why
don't they try?

'I'll just call Mother'
'Better give George a ring'
Can't they call another
day? No wonder they're too busy
to do anything.

The new one
sits in the hall,
chirrups away
like an electric mouse,
busy all day,
ruling the house.

Grownups moan
about the telephone,
upstairs, downstairs,
out of beds and armchairs,
never see a programme through:
what can they do?

'Not that phone again' they shout.

Why don't they have it taken out?

Poem for a Little Prince

Away in a Palace, no crib for *his* bed,
The little Prince Henry lays down his sweet head;
A radiant mother and servants in rows,
Detectives to follow wherever he goes.

The cameras are whirring, the baby awakes,
But little Prince Henry no crying he makes:
No magical kiss and no dragons to slay,
Young Harry will marry a Princess one day.

Beauty to Beast

for Carol Ann Duffy

"Beauty will now say a few words . . ."

1.
It's all very well for her.
I mean, it's fun being a Beast,
Roaming the woods
until goodness knows what time,
coming home with feathers all round her mouth.

2.
Hopeless I follow
the trail of broken mirrors
along the endless corridors
of your Palace. Broken glass
and last year's leaves
crunch under my feet.
I cannot see my face.

Beast, you are my mirror.

3.
Beauty is in the eye of
the Beast, the beholder:

Beauty is as Beast does.

4.
It's boring.

Standing here,
covered in oil,
flexing my muscles,
practising being beautiful.

It's *boring*.

5.
Sing for me, dark and lonely Beast,
Sing me your ancient song.
Sing of your dark and lonely fate,
Sing of your ancient wrong.

6.
An April Fool in October
you mistake my pity for affection.

No birds sing beside the sullen lake.
Beast, have mercy upon me.

7.
It's ridiculous.

The spotlight
teetering along this platform
a crown   a sash
MR FAIRYLAND indeed
What am I doing here?
Who will laugh now?

It's ridiculous.

8.
Chocolate and gingerbread
Chocolate and gingerbread
Curse the stone heart
That's covered in icing.

33

9.
Cottagelights through the snow
sugar-plum bright and whiteness everywhere,
the smell of pine-needles.
Lonely as the fairy
on top of the Christmas-tree,
I watch her fumble with presents.

10.
I have guessed your name.

A year here and I wait
At the enchanted gate.
Beast, I cannot leave you.

Take this rose.

Wait.

Best Friends

It's Susan I talk to not Tracey,
Before that I sat next to Jane;
I used to be best friends with Lynda
But these days I think she's a pain.

Natasha's all right in small doses,
I meet Mandy sometimes in town;
I'm jealous of Annabel's pony
And I don't like Nicola's frown.

I used to go skating with Catherine,
Before that I went there with Ruth;
And Kate's so much better at trampoline:
She's a showoff, to tell you the truth.

I think that I'm going off Susan,
She borrowed my comb yesterday;
I *think* I might sit next to Tracey,
She's my nearly best friend: she's OK.

Nightmare Cemetery

Don't go down with me today
to Nightmare Cemetery
You don't know what you'll see today
in Nightmare Cemetery

Don't go through the gates today
to Nightmare Cemetery
You don't know what waits today
in Nightmare Cemetery

Don't go down the lane today
to Nightmare Cemetery
There you might remain today
in Nightmare Cemetery

Don't go down the road today
to Nightmare Cemetery
Haunt of bat and toad today
in Nightmare Cemetery

The sun will never shine today
in Nightmare Cemetery
Horrors wait in line today
in Nightmare Cemetery

Close the gates and step inside
Much too late to try and hide
Hear the hinges creak with glee
I'll be waiting, just you see,
You're here forever, just like me
in Nightmare Cemetery.

Morning Break

Eleven O'Clock:
seagulls noisy as children
pick up crisps from the empty playground.

Square Meal

He kept a pet hyena
And then he bought a flock
He fed them all on Oxo cubes
And made a laughing stock.

Elephants

An elephant
can't jump
(not even
a little one)
he'd probably go
all the way through
to Australia;
he must feel a bit
of a failure.

On the other hand,
a whale can jump
right out of the water.
A camel can lift his hump
above the desert sands.
Emus and yaks
leap in the air
without a care.
Even a hippopotamus
won't sink to the bottomless
depths of the river,
even though his weight
makes the ground quiver
when he lands.

As for the chimpanzee
he can land on his hands
if he wants to.

But what can the poor elephant do?

He has to flap his ears for joy
He has to wade through puddles
He has to wave his trunk with fright
which causes endless muddles.

His feet firmly on the ground,
an elephant
(not even
a little one)
can't jump, you see,
unlike you
or me
(or even
a flea).

Sammy the Flying Piglet

See him fly!
See him fly!
See the piglet in the sky!

Off to Athens
Off to Rome
Over France then straight back home
for tea:
thought Sammy 'This is the life
for me'

Even before
he ever flew
little Sammy always knew
he only had to try
and one day
he'd fly.

'What?
Pigs fly?
When Nelson gets his eye
back' his mother would grunt
'One day' thought Sammy,
the runt of the litter,
'I'll show them'

See him fly!
See him fly!
A piglet hurtling
across the sky –
Eight miles high!

Over valleys, over hills,
dodging pylons, dodging mills,
chasing cattle, scaring sheep,
loop the loop
then straight back home
to sleep.

All the others on the farm
viewed his skills with some alarm
'Heavens! What's he doing now?
Bless us all!' said the oldest cow
'A flying pig? Whatever next?'
Even his brothers felt quite vexed
standing earthbound by their trough
while the smallest pig took off.

See him fly!
See him fly!
That's our Sammy
in the sky!
Heaven knows why!

Off to Athens
Off to Rome
Over Spain and then again
back home:
thought Sammy 'This is the life
for me

I'm free!

Whoopee!'

Out of Line
for the children of Rossmore Junior School

Our computer keeps going on the blink
What use is a computer
That can't even think
Straight?

Our stupid computer
Can't even spell
I doubt if he can even tell
The time.

That computer
Can't get anything right
Doesn't even know a bark
From a byte.

What use is a computer
That can't find its bits?
I think it's losing
Its wits.

Our computer
Can hardly get on-line.
I'm glad it's the school's
Not mine.

Visitor

1.
Prepare to decelerate.

I haven't seen these feet for years:
they look young.

2.
It is blue, this place
and, nearer, green also.
The only star that gives them light
appears to be yellow.

3.
Crowds of them have turned out
to watch me land.

Oh, goodness, they're *pink*
and they've only got two of each!

4.
How can they see
without antennae?

5.
I think they're trying to welcome me.

Some of them
are putting bits of burnt dead things
into a hole in the middle of their heads
Ugh!

6.
I'm off.

Can't wait to get my tentacles on the control-panel.

What a relief
to get back to where people are *normal*.

Africa

I asked for another piece of cake
And suddenly thought
Of the faces I see on TV
Of the children of Africa
Stomachs full of emptiness
Little legs like sugarcanes
Swarms of flies round big sad eyes.

Early Spring

Daffodils shiver,
huddle away from the wind,
like people waiting at a bus-stop.

Poem for a Windy Day

for the children of
Market Drayton Junior School

Before it got to the end of the first
line

the poem
        blew
                . away
sailed
            across the grass
                            over

two classrooms
and a fence,
two lines of washing,
three allotments,
and finished
                just before the last line
sheltering a goldfish in an ornamental pond.

Night Comics

for Michael Kustow

Hee-hee. I should get plenty of presents in this!
I got sneezing powder A A A A CHOO!
ERK. I'm locked in!
CRUMBS. If only I hadn't crocked my ankle!
But first I'll walk across the ice – AARGH!
HAW. HAW. HAW.
You've won um feed
Puff. Pant. Seven-and-a-half minutes! Gasp!
Coo. King Biffeau the Conqueror
YAHOO! Teacher's retiring!
SWISH! SLURP! SNARL! GNASH!
Look at that lovely money!
BONK! OOF! YOWP!
UNLOAD THE GRUB!
SOON HAVE YOU OUT, TEACHER
Mm. Lovely smell!
Shriek! A mouse!
Wow! I've stepped on a tube of paint!
Cease this nonsense and return to school at once!
WHACK!

(cut-up from one issue of
The Beano)

58

Blood Brothers

Jim Dracula and Albert Frankenstein
live on a council estate near Crewe.
The two work on the night shift,
and often travel in together on the bus.
Jim carries his blood sandwiches
in a blue plastic lunchbox, and Albert
always has a flask of steaming, bright green liquid.
Jim runs a one-man transfusion service;
Albert works on the assembly-line
in a body factory.

'I've always been clever with my hands,'
says Albert
'It's a matter of taste, I suppose,'
says Jim,
licking his lips.

Jim Dracula and Albert Frankenstein
like to roam but are happiest at home
with their work, and can't wait to get back.
Jim has packed his wooden stake and bit of
    Cheshire soil
in a brand new vinyl coffin,
ready for his package-tour of Transylvania.
Albert has dozed off
while reading his manual of spare-part surgery
in a laboratory high in the mountains.

Jim Dracula and Albert Frankenstein
will be back to the old routine next week,
off to work as the sun sets,
and tucked up in the vault by breakfast-time;
down to the graveyard for fresh supplies,
or fluttering up the front of tower-blocks.

'I haven't had a bite all day,'
says Jim
'Give us a hand,'
says Albert,
'This one's got one foot
in the grave.'

Not Me!

Every little girl would like to be
the fairy on the Christmas tree
except me.
I'd rather be
a Kung-Fu fighter like Bruce Lee.

Every little girl would like to be
The Queen of the May
and reign for a day.
I'd rather stow away
and hitch-hike across the USA.

Every little girl would like to be
a bridesmaid or a bride;
not me. I'd rather ride
a motorbike. Or hide
inside a pirate's cave. Or save
a penalty-kick at Wembley.
Or have the Secret Service send me
on missions as a spy. Or fly
a shuttle into space. Or race
against Sebastian Coe. I know
what *other* little girls would like to be

Not me!

Dawn Chorus

If I were a blackbird
I'd whistle and sing
And stay in bed
Until eleven in the morning.

Any Prince to Any Princess

August is coming
and the goose, I'm afraid,
is getting fat.
There have been
no golden eggs for some months now.
Straw has fallen well below market price
despite my frantic spinning
and the sedge is,
as you rightly point out,
withered.

I can't imagine how the pea
got under your mattress. I apologize
humbly. The chambermaid has, of course,
been sacked. As has the frog footman.
I understand that, during my recent fact-finding
                      tour of the Golden River,
despite your nightly unavailing efforts,
he remained obstinately
froggish.

I hope that the Three Wishes granted by the
                                    General Assembly
will go some way towards redressing
this unfortunate recent sequence of events.
The fall in output from the shoe-factory, for
                                    example:
no one could have foreseen the work-to-rule
by the National Union of Elves. Not to mention
                                    the fact
that the court has been fast asleep
for the last six and a half years.
The matter of the poisoned apple has been taken
                                    up
by the Board of Trade: I think I can assure you
the incident will not be
repeated.

I can quite understand, in the circumstances,
your reluctance to let down
your golden tresses. However
I feel I must point out
that the weather isn't getting any better
and I already have a nasty chill
from waiting at the base
of the White Tower. You must see
the absurdity of the situation.

Some of the courtiers are beginning to talk,
not to mention the humble villagers.
It's been three weeks now, and not even
a word.

Princess,
a cold, black wind
howls through our empty palace.
Dead leaves litter the bedchamber;
the mirror on the wall hasn't said a thing
since you left. I can only ask,
bearing all this in mind,
that you think again,

let down your hair,

reconsider.

Newsflash

Reports are just coming in that . . .

THE TOYS HAVE TAKEN OVER TOYTOWN!
After fierce fighting in the hills above Nutwood
The Famous Five have succeeded in capturing the
                                                    Chalet School
and have linked up with forces
led by Algy the Pug and Rupert Bear.
Tintin and Captain Haddock,
after making the perilous approach by sea,
have taken the harbour without a struggle.

Noddy and Big Ears
lead the triumphal motorcade down the High Street
followed by the tramp tramp tramp of feet
of the Mister Men. Paddington Bear
and The Railway Children
ride Thomas the Tank Engine.

Mr Quelch and Ernest the Policeman
have fled into exile.

Postman Pat has taken over the Radio Station,
broadcasts an appeal for calm to the nation,
proclaims a new democratic regime,
free sweets for all,
the abolition of bedtime.

As dusk falls on riot-torn Toytown
the air is filled with laughter,
the munching of chocolate,
and the soft sound of teddybears,
dancing.

Just Imagine . . .

Just imagine,
a rabbit,
a single, solitary rabbit,
living on a traffic-island
in the middle of a city!

Tanker-lorries, taxis, big green buses
thunder round his little kingdom:
if you sit on the top deck you might just see him,
licking his paws or eating a tulip.

The Council made a garden
in the middle of the traffic-island
daffodils and azaleas,
hollyhocks and chrysanthemums
grow there in season,
even a coat-of-arms made out of flowers.

But I'm *sure* they didn't plant
a rabbit,
a single, solitary rabbit,
in a burrow
in the middle of a great big traffic-island
in the middle of a city,
the roar of traffic and the smell of petrol-fumes
all around his little home.

So how did he get there?

I can't imagine.

Can you?

George the Crab
and Lewis the Lobster

Lives of shellfish all remind us
We should make our life sublime
And, departing, leave behind us
Claw-prints on the sands of time.

George the crab
Is a fine but rather under-rated poet,
the pride of Weymouth Bay.
On the other hand, some say
that Lewis the lobster
who hails from Camber Sands,
would win claws down
as a writer of verse.

Quarrels, and worse, broke out
between father and daughter, mother and son,
in rock-pools all along the coast.

Most of the shrimps and some of the oysters
spoke highly of Lewis. The vast majority
of cockles and mussels plumped
for George. His 'Ode to a Lobster-Pot'
was said by some to be in bad taste, a waste
of time. Lewis' rhyme
'I wandered lonely as a crab'
was criticised too.

But few
realised what friends the two
were. Why, at dusk on many an evening
you can see them wander sideways
claw-in-claw along the beach,
each murmuring a line or two,
until the sun sets
at the end of the poem
and they pause for a little drink.

Shellfish
are not as selfish
as people think.

Haiku

hai-ku
    hai-ku
        hai-
coo the pigeons

in springtime
    -ku
       hai-ku
           hai-ku.

Lullaby

Imagine being asleep in the deep
Counting whales instead of sheep.

Conversation on a Garden Wall

Move over, you've got all the bricks with the sun on.

Oh, all right. Mind you, I was here first.

He came round after me again last night.
Right up to the back door.

Really? He's persistent, I'll say that for him.

I'll say. Anyway, they chased him away.

How are yours treating you?

Not too bad, really.
They're a bit careful with the milk.

Oh, mine are all right about that. They're a bit
unimaginative with my food, though. Last week
I had the same meal every day.

You don't say. The food's OK. It's a real pain
being pushed out in the rain. Every night, rain or
snow, out I go.

Me, too. Look, here he is back again.

Cheek. Pretend to take no notice.

At least you've got a quiet place with none of those small ones around. I hardly get a minute.

That's true. All mine do is sit in front of a little box with tiny ones inside it.

Mine do too. It's the only peace I get.

And one of them pushes that noisy thing
round the floor every day.

Terrible, isn't it? Mind you,
mine only does it once or twice a week.

You're lucky. Oh, the sun's gone in.

Yes, time for a stroll. I'll jump down and
just sort of walk past him, accidentally.

Accidentally on purpose, you mean.
See you round.

Yes, see you around. I'll tell you one thing, though.

What's that?

It's a good job they can't talk,
isn't it?

Rebel without a Sword

Spike the short sharp shark
was a swordfish who never grew
after running into a coral reef for a lark
when he was two. Which put his sword
out of joint. There was merriment
all along the ocean floor. 'How quaint'
'I never saw the like' 'Like a sawfish
without a saw' 'He's like a sawn-off
shark' 'Or a dogfish without a bark'
and the like. Poor Spike
moved to another part of the sea,
where he passed himself off
as a shark. In the dark
you couldn't tell the difference.
His strong jaws and long nose
were much admired by lady sharks.
He basks in their attentions,
and never mentions the past.
'I may be a short sharp shark'
says Spike, 'But you must admit
I've got a point.'

Blue Christmas

I'm having a lousy Christmas
Not even a robin in sight,
There's a great big hole in my stocking,
and I've just fused the Christmas tree lights.

The dog is away in the manger,
Even the pudding won't light;
Singing Merry Christmas
On this all-too-silent night.

Good King Wenceslas looked out
Over a year ago:
How can I follow his footsteps
When there isn't any snow?

The mistletoe's getting all dusty
With no one there to kiss,
Even the mince pies taste musty:
Can New Year be worse than this?

The Phantom Lollipop Lady

The phantom lollipop lady
haunts the crossroads
where the old school used to be;
they closed it down in 1973.

The old lollipop lady
loved her job, and stood there
for seven years altogether,
no matter how bad the weather.

When they pulled the old school down
she still stood there every day:
a pocketful of sweets for the little ones,
smiles and a joke for the big ones.

One day the lollipop lady
was taken away to hospital.
Without her standing there
the corner looked, somehow, bare.

After a month and two operations
the lollipop lady died;
the children felt something missing:
she had made her final crossing.

Now if you go down alone at dusk
just before the streetlights go on,
look closely at the corner over there:
in the shadows by the lamp-post you'll see her.

Helping phantom children across the street,
holding up the traffic with a ghostly hand;
at the twilight crossing where four roads meet
the phantom lollipop lady stands.